For my wonderful mother.

—CBE

www.mascotbooks.com

Petey Rex and the Designated Hitter

©2016 Christopher Burke. All Rights Reserved. No part of this publication
may be reproduced, stored in a retrieval system or transmitted in any
form by any means electronic, mechanical, or photocopying, recording or
otherwise without the permission of the author.

For more information, please contact:
Mascot Books
560 Herndon Parkway #120
Herndon, VA 20170
info@mascotbooks.com

Library of Congress Control Number: 2016902780

CPSIA Code: PRT0516A
ISBN-13: 978-1-63177-661-8

Printed in the United States

Petey Rex and the DESIGNATED HITTER

by Christopher Burke · Illustrated by Helena Crevel

Petey Rex was the only Tyrannosaurus on an island full of Pterodactyls.

He never quite fit in because he was so much bigger and different from the Pterodactyls.

Petey was especially sad when they played baseball.

He couldn't swing the bat because of his little arms, and all the Pterodactyls poked fun at him when he tried to hit the ball.

So Petey just sat out and watched,
alone on the island of Pterodactyls.

Tommy was the smallest Pterodactyl on the island.

He never quite fit in because he was smaller than the other Pterodactyls and had to wear glasses.

Tommy also felt sad when he watched the others play baseball.

He wasn't tall enough to catch the balls in the outfield, and even though he worked hard, the other Pterodactyls poked fun at him every time he tried.

So Tommy just sat out and watched, alone on the island of Pterodactyls.

One day as they were watching the other Pterodactyls play, a deep foul ball went zooming right past Petey. Tommy saw it and yelled, **"Catch it!"**

Petey took two steps and a leap and caught it right in his mouth.

"Spit out now, mini-arms!" called one of the Pterodactyls. Everyone laughed.

Petey spit it out, and headed
home with his head hanging low.

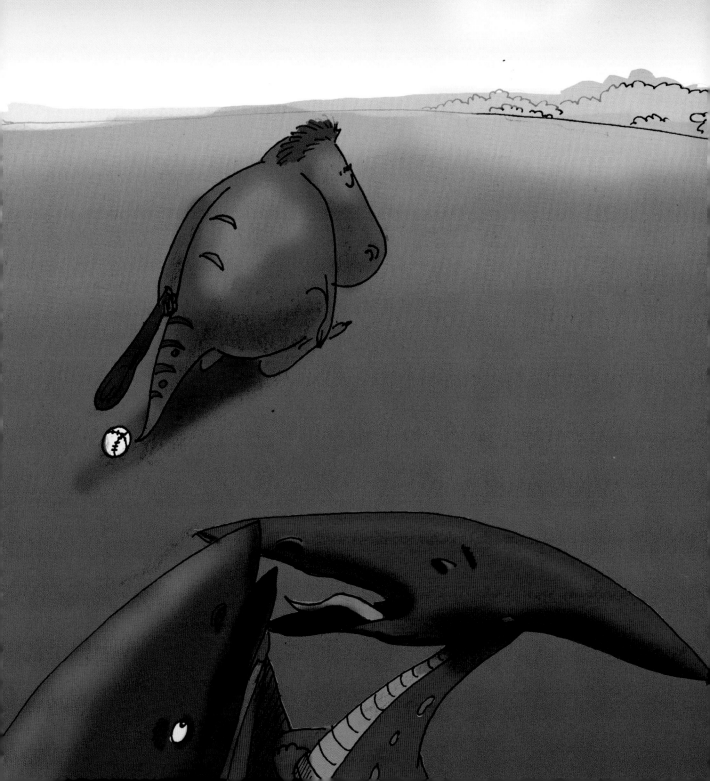

"Hey man, you can really catch!"
Tommy called after Petey. "Why don't you play?"

"You know why," Petey growled. "I can't hit the ball with my little arms. Why don't you play?"

"I can't get to all the balls with my little legs," replied Tommy.

"Wait a second," said Tommy, jumping to his feet. "Why don't you catch the balls and I'll hit them?"

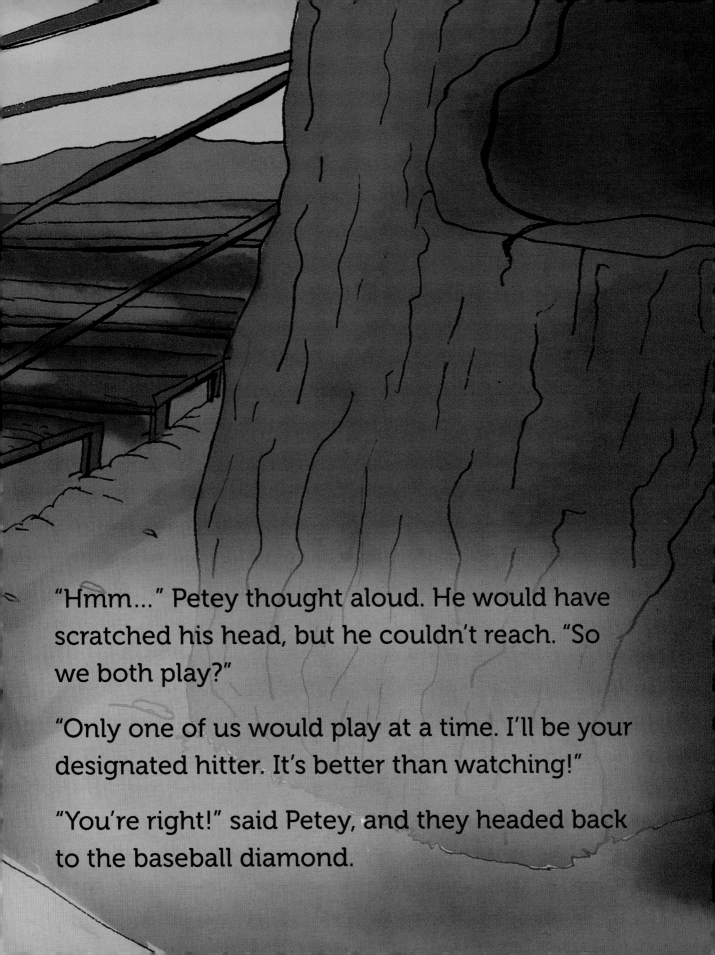

"Hmm..." Petey thought aloud. He would have scratched his head, but he couldn't reach. "So we both play?"

"Only one of us would play at a time. I'll be your designated hitter. It's better than watching!"

"You're right!" said Petey, and they headed back to the baseball diamond.

They went to every team and asked if they could play. But everyone said...

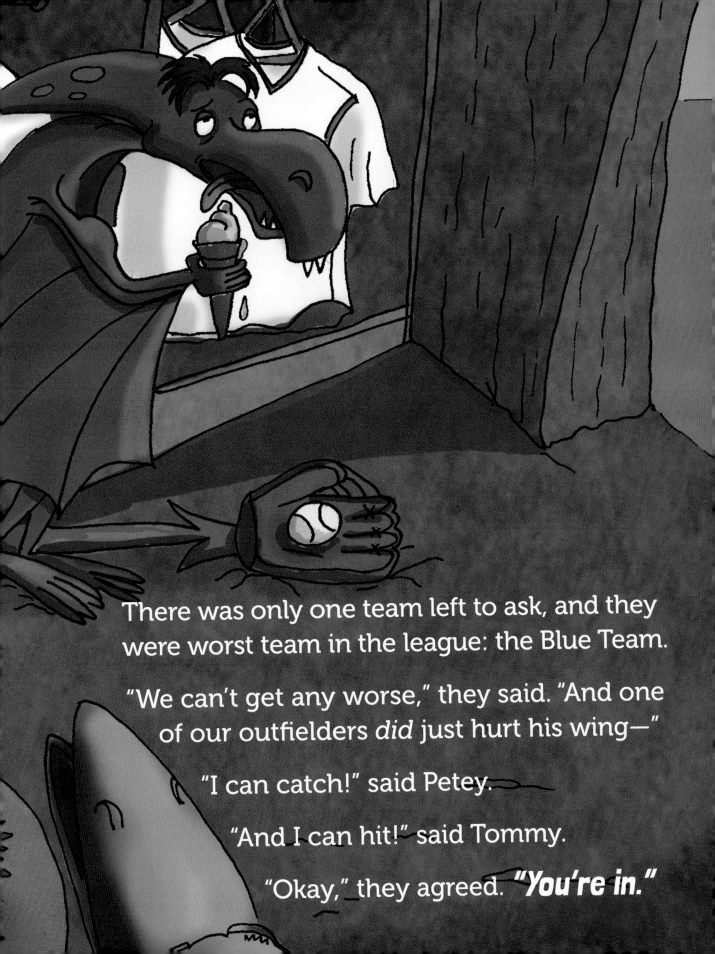

There was only one team left to ask, and they were worst team in the league: the Blue Team.

"We can't get any worse," they said. "And one of our outfielders *did* just hurt his wing—"

"I can catch!" said Petey.

"And I can hit!" said Tommy.

"Okay," they agreed. ***"You're in."***

Petey played in the outfield
and caught every ball...

Together they helped the Blue Team
win the last three games of the season.
They were the heroes!

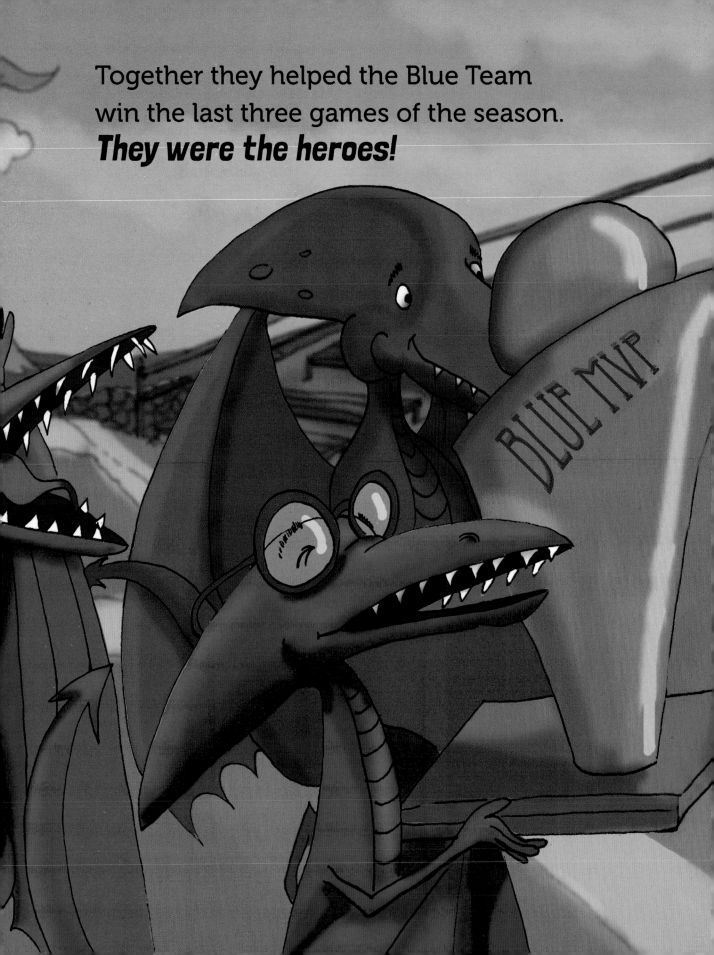

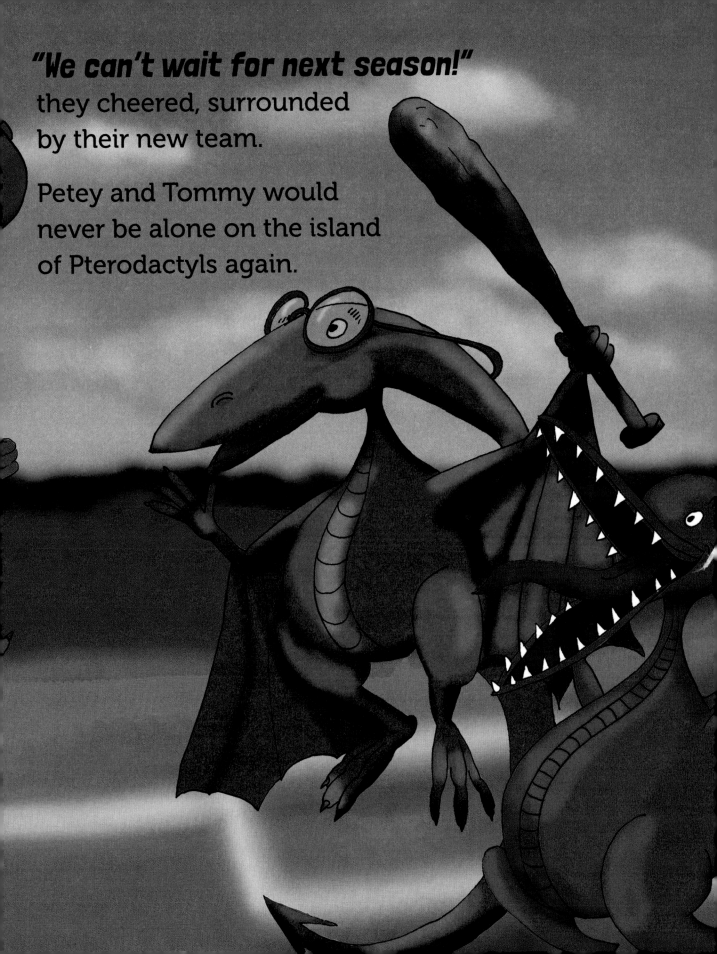

"**We can't wait for next season!**" they cheered, surrounded by their new team.

Petey and Tommy would never be alone on the island of Pterodactyls again.

Christopher Burke is a veteran submariner and graduate of Duke University. *Petey Rex and the Designated Hitter* is his first children's book, inspired by his two younger brothers and a desire to teach important lessons at an early age. "You're never too young to learn the concepts of dreaming big, giving it your all, and never giving up!" He brings his stories to life from his home in Austin, Texas.